CAT AT BAT

by John Stadler

PUFFIN BOOKS

PUFFIN BOOKS
Published by the Penguin Group
Penguin Books USA Inc., 375 Hudson Street, New York, New York 10014, U.S.A.
Penguin Books Ltd, 27 Wrights Lane, London W8 5TZ, England
Penguin Books Australia Ltd, Ringwood, Victoria, Australia
Penguin Books Canada Ltd, 10 Alcorn Avenue, Toronto, Ontario, Canada M4V 3B2
Penguin Books (N.Z.) Ltd, 182–190 Wairau Road, Auckland 10, New Zealand

Penguin Books Ltd, Registered Offices: Harmondsworth, Middlesex, England

First published in the United States of America by E. P. Dutton, 1979
Published in a Puffin Easy-to-Read edition, 1995

1 3 5 7 9 10 8 6 4 2

The Library of Congress has cataloged the E. P. Dutton edition as follows:
Stadler, John.
Cat at bat.
Summary: Presents fourteen rhymed verses describing the
activities of animals such as "A duck and his truck are stuck."
1. English language—Rhyme—Juvenile literature.
[1. Animals—Poetry. 2. American poetry.] I. Title.
PE1517.S7   1988   811'.54 87-36400   ISBN 0-525-44416-5

Puffin Easy-to-Read ISBN 0-14-037005-6

Reading Level 2.8

to Mom, Dad, Anne, and Ric

an affectionate acknowledgment
to Dorothea von Elbe and Linda Spencer
for their help

A cat

is up

at bat.

A dog

is on a log

with a hog.

Two nice

mice

are on the ice.

A cub

is in a tub

for a scrub.

A fish

on a dish

has a wish.

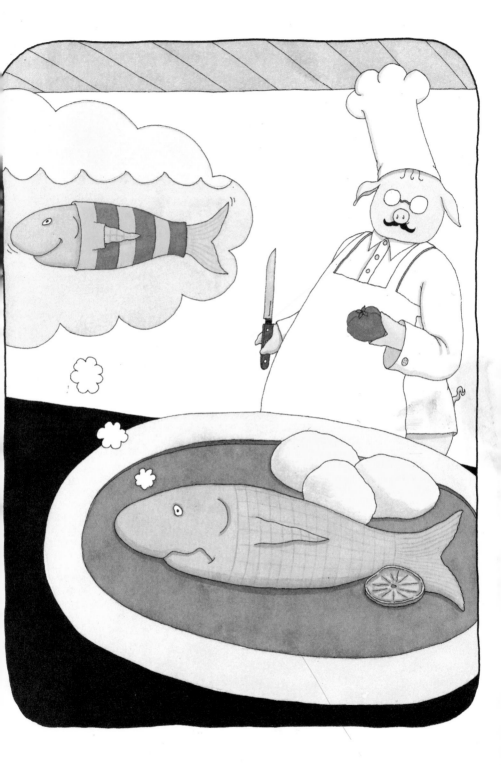

A fox

will box

an ox.

A mole

is on a pole

below a hole.

A duck

and his truck

are stuck.

A snail

is on a tail

with the mail.

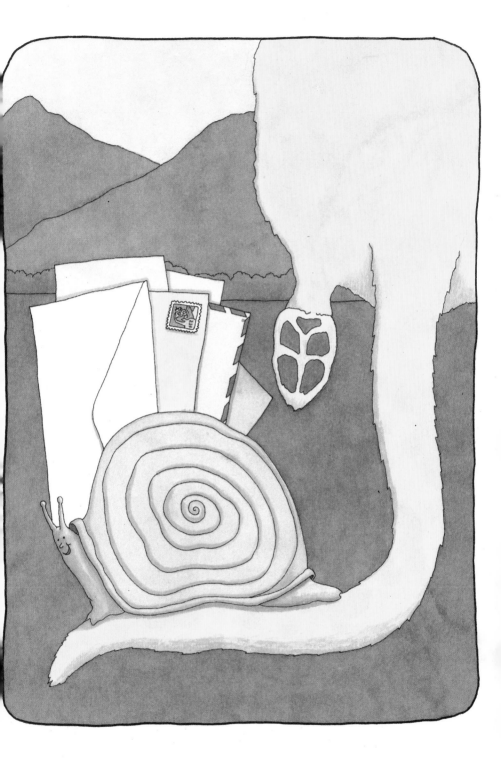

A sheep

is deep

in sleep.

A seal

tries to steal

a meal.

A skunk

carries a trunk

with a chipmunk.

A crow

has a bow

and arrow.

A crocodile

runs a mile

with a smile.